Humpty Dumpty
and friends

Miles
KeLLY

First published in 2011 by Miles Kelly Publishing Ltd
Harding's Barn, Bardfield End Green, Thaxted, Essex, CM6 3PX, UK

This edition published 2012 for Index Books

4 6 8 10 9 7 5

Publishing Director Belinda Gallagher
Creative Director Jo Cowan
Editor Sarah Parkin
Cover/Junior Designer Kayleigh Allen
Production Manager Elizabeth Collins
Reprographics Stephan Davis, Ian Paulyn
Assets Lorraine King

ISBN 978-1-84810-410-5

Printed in China

British Library Cataloguing-in-Publication Data
A catalogue record for this book is available from the British Library

ACKNOWLEDGEMENTS

Artworks are from the Miles Kelly Artwork Bank
Cover artist: Rosalind Beardshaw

Made with paper from a sustainable forest

www.mileskelly.net
info@mileskelly.net
www.factsforprojects.com

Contents

One Potato

One potato, two potato,
Three potato, four,
Five potato, six potato,
Seven potato more.

Take turns with your partner in placing one fist on top of another to build a tower.

When you reach seven start again.

The Crocodile

If you should meet a crocodile
Don't take a stick and poke him.
Ignore the welcome in his smile,
Be careful not to stroke him.

For as he sleeps upon the Nile,
He thinner gets and thinner;
So whene'er you meet a crocodile
He's ready for his dinner.

Yankee Doodle

Yankee Doodle came to town,
Riding on a pony;
He stuck a feather in his cap
And called it macaroni.

Yankee doodle, doodle do,
Yankee doodle dandy,
All the lasses are so smart,
And sweet as sugar candy.

Cock a Doodle Doo

Cock a doodle doo!
My dame has lost her shoe;
My master's lost his
Fiddling stick
And doesn't know
what to do.

Rapunzel

A retelling from the original fairytale
by the Brothers Grimm

Once upon a time there lived a man and his wife who for years and years had wanted a child. One day the wife was looking sadly out of the window. Winter was coming but in the next door garden, which was surrounded by a huge great wall, she could just see rows and rows of delicious-looking vegetables. In particular, she could see a huge bunch of rapunzel, a special kind of lettuce. Her mouth watered, it looked so fresh and green.

"Husband, I shall not rest until I have some of that rapunzel growing next door," she whispered.

The husband clambered over the wall and quickly picked a small bunch, which he took back to his wife. She made it into a salad, and ate it all up. But the next day, all she could think of was how delicious it had been so she asked him to pick her some more.

He clambered over the wall, and was picking a small bunch of the rapunzel when a voice behind him hissed, "So you are the one who has been stealing my rapunzel!"

When he spun round, there stood a witch
and she looked very angry indeed. The
husband was terrified, but he tried to
explain that his wife had been desperate for
fresh leaves for her salad.

"You may take all the leaves you require
then, but you must give me your first child
when she is born," smiled the witch, and it
was not a nice smile. The husband was
greatly relieved, however, for he knew that

there was little chance of his wife ever having a daughter so he fled back over the wall, clutching the bunch of rapunzel. He did not tell his wife of his meeting with the witch for he thought it would only frighten her, and he soon forgot all about his adventure.

But it all came back to him when nine months later his wife gave birth to a beautiful baby girl. No sooner had she laid the baby in her cradle, than the witch appeared to claim the child. The wife wept, the husband pleaded but nothing could persuade the witch to forget the husband's awful promise, and so she took the tiny baby away.

The witch called the baby Rapunzel. She grew into a beautiful girl with long, long hair as fine as spun gold. When she was sixteen, the witch took Rapunzel and locked her in a tall tower so no one would see how beautiful she was. The witch threw away the key to the tower, and so whenever she wanted to visit Rapunzel she would call out, "Rapunzel, Rapunzel, let down your hair," and Rapunzel would throw her golden plait of hair out of the window at the top of the tower so the witch could slowly scramble up.

Now one day it happened that a handsome young prince was riding through the woods. He heard the witch call out to Rapunzel and he watched her climb up the tower. After the witch had gone, the prince came to the bottom of the tower and he called up, "Rapunzel, Rapunzel, let down your hair," and he climbed quickly up the shining golden plait. You can imagine Rapunzel's astonishment when she saw the handsome prince standing in front of her but she was soon laughing at his stories. When he left, he promised to come again the next day, and he did. And the next, and the next, and soon they had fallen in love with each other.

One day as the witch clambered up, Rapunzel exclaimed, "You are slow! The prince doesn't take nearly as long to climb up the tower," but no

sooner were the words out of her mouth than she realized her terrible mistake. The witch seized the long, long golden plait and cut it off. She drove Rapunzel far, far away from the tower, and then sat down to await the prince. When the witch heard him calling, she threw the golden plait out of the window. Imagine the prince's dismay when he sprang into the room only to discover the horrible witch instead of his beautiful Rapunzel! When the witch told him he would never see his Rapunzel again, in his grief he flung himself out of the tower. He fell into some brambles that scratched his eyes so he could no longer see.

And thus he wandered the land, always asking if anyone had seen his Rapunzel. After seven long years, he came to the place where she had hidden herself away. As he stumbled down the road, Rapunzel recognized him, and with a great cry of joy she ran up to him and took him gently by the hand to her little cottage in the woods. As she washed his face, two of her tears fell on the prince's eyes and his sight came back. And so they went back to his palace and lived happily ever after. The witch, you will be pleased to hear, had not been able to get down from the tower, so she did NOT live happily ever after!

Little Robin Redbreast

Little Robin Redbreast sat upon a tree,
Up went Pussy-cat, down went he,
Down came Pussy-cat, away Robin ran,
Says little Robin Redbreast,
"Catch me if you can!"

Little Robin Redbreast
jumped upon a spade,
Pussy-cat jumped after him,
and then he was afraid.
Little Robin chirped and sang,
and what did Pussy say?
Pussy-cat said, "Mew, mew, mew,"
and Robin flew away.

Humpty Dumpty

Humpty Dumpty sat on a wall,
Humpty Dumpty had a great fall;
All the king's horses and all the king's men
Couldn't put Humpty together again.

Five Little Pussy Cats

Five little pussy cats
playing near the door;
One ran and hid inside
And then there were four.

Four little pussy cats
underneath a tree;
One heard a dog bark
And then there were three.

Three little pussy cats
thinking what to do;
One saw a little bird
And then there were two.

Two little pussy cats
sitting in the sun;
One ran to catch his tail
And then there was one.

One little pussy cat
looking for some fun;
He saw a butterfly
And then there was none.

Jack be Nimble

Jack be nimble,
Jack be quick,
Jack jump over the candlestick.

Snow White and the Seven Dwarfs

A retelling from the original tale
by the Brothers Grimm

The queen was sitting at the window sewing, and thinking about her baby who would soon be born. As she sewed she pricked her finger, and blood fell on the snow by the ebony window ledge.

"I wish that my daughter be as white as snow, as black as ebony and as red as blood," she said to herself, and so it happened. Her daughter had skin as white as snow, lips as red as blood and hair as black as ebony, so she was called Snow White. But the queen died and the king married again. His new wife had a cold heart, and she did not love Snow White.

Every morning the new queen would look into her magic mirror and say, "Mirror, mirror on the wall, who is fairest in the land?"

And the mirror would always reply, "Thou, oh queen, thou art fairest in the land."

So the queen was content. Seven years passed and Snow White grew into a lovely young girl.

One morning the queen looked

into her mirror, but the mirror's reply filled her with a deep envy.

"Thou, oh queen, thou art indeed fair. But Snow White is the fairest in the land."

She ordered her woodsman to kill Snow White. But he could not bear to do such a wicked deed so he hid Snow White deep in the forest. Snow White wandered about until she was utterly weary.

Suddenly, she caught sight of a light through the trees in the distance. It came from a little house. The door swung open at her touch, so she stepped inside. A scrubbed wooden table was set, with seven plates and seven cups. Seven little chairs were

ranged round the fireplace, and along the back wall there were seven little beds, each with a brightly coloured blanket.

There was a basket of logs beside the fireplace, and Snow White soon had a fire going. She sat in one of the little chairs and before long was fast asleep.

The cottage belonged to seven dwarfs and when they came home that evening, they were worried to discover Snow White fast asleep. They tiptoed round preparing their supper, but as the wonderful smell of stew filled the room, Snow White awoke with a start. She was surprised to see seven little faces looking at her, but soon she was telling them how she came to be in the forest. They were very angry when they heard about the wicked queen.

"Might I stay with you?" asked Snow White. "I could look after you, and have supper ready for you every night."

The dwarfs were delighted with this suggestion, and immediately set about making Snow White her own chair by the fireside and her own bed.

Back in the castle, the queen looked into her mirror in the morning, and asked,

"Mirror, mirror on the wall, who is fairest in the land?"

The mirror replied, "Thou, oh queen, thou art indeed fair. But Snow White with the seven dwarfs does dwell and she is fairest in the land."

The wicked queen disguised herself as an old pedlar, and searched out the dwarfs' cottage. Snow White did not recognize the queen and invited her in.

"Goodness me, you need new laces for your dress," said the old woman, and she pulled the new laces so tightly that Snow White was unable to breathe.

When the dwarfs came home that evening, they were horrified to discover Snow White lying on the floor as if dead.

They lifted her up and saw the laces. They cut the tight cord and the colour came back to Snow White's cheeks.

"The queen will stop at nothing," they cried. "You must not let anyone indoors."

The queen looked in her mirror the next morning and went white with rage when it said Snow White was still the fairest in the land. She disguised herself as a gypsy, selling wooden combs and went to the dwarfs' cottage. Snow White would not open the door. But the gypsy passed a comb through the window, and the second it touched her hair, Snow White fainted.

When the dwarfs came home and found Snow White, they pulled the poisoned comb from her hair, and she sat up. They pleaded with her to be more careful the next morning.

When a farmer's wife appeared at the door trying to sell apples, Snow White would not even open the window.

"Why, anyone would think I was trying to poison you," said the farmer's wife, who was the wicked queen in disguise.

"I only want to give you some apples. Look how juicy they are!" and she took a big bite out of one.

Snow White thought it must be all right and she took the apple. But the queen had poisoned it on one side only, and the minute Snow White took a bite she fell down dead.

This time when the dwarfs came home, there was nothing they could do. They could not bear to bury her in the cold earth so they placed her in a glass coffin. They wrote her name on the side and put the coffin in a sheltered part of the forest.

When the queen looked into her mirror the next morning, it gave her the answer she wanted.

"Thou, oh queen, thou art fairest in the land."

Years passed, and Snow White lay in her coffin. The dwarfs watched over her, and one day they found a young prince kneeling by the side of the glass coffin. He had fallen in love with Snow White the moment he had set eyes on her. When the dwarfs saw how deeply the prince felt about their beloved Snow White, they agreed that he take the glass coffin to his palace.

As the prince lifted the glass coffin, the piece of poisoned apple flew from her lips, and Snow White opened her eyes. She saw the prince, and her faithful dwarfs and she cried, "Where am I? What has happened?"

There was huge excitement as everyone tried to talk at once. The prince asked Snow White to marry him. She agreed as long as the dwarfs could come and live at the palace as well, and they all lived happily ever after.

But what of the queen? She looked in her mirror the morning Snow White and the prince were to be married.

"Mirror, mirror on the wall, who is fairest in the land?"

The mirror replied, "Snow White, oh queen, Snow White who marries her prince today, she is fairest in the land."

The queen was so ugly in her rage that the mirror cracked and she was never able to look in it again!

Little Boy Blue

Little Boy Blue,
Come blow your horn,
The sheep's in the
meadow,
The cow's in
the corn.

But where is the boy
Who looks after the sheep?
He's under a haystack,
Fast asleep.

"Will you wake him?"
"No, not I,
For if I do,
He's sure to cry."

Star Light, Star Bright

Star light, star bright,
First star I see tonight,
I wish I may, I wish I might,
Have the wish I wish tonight.